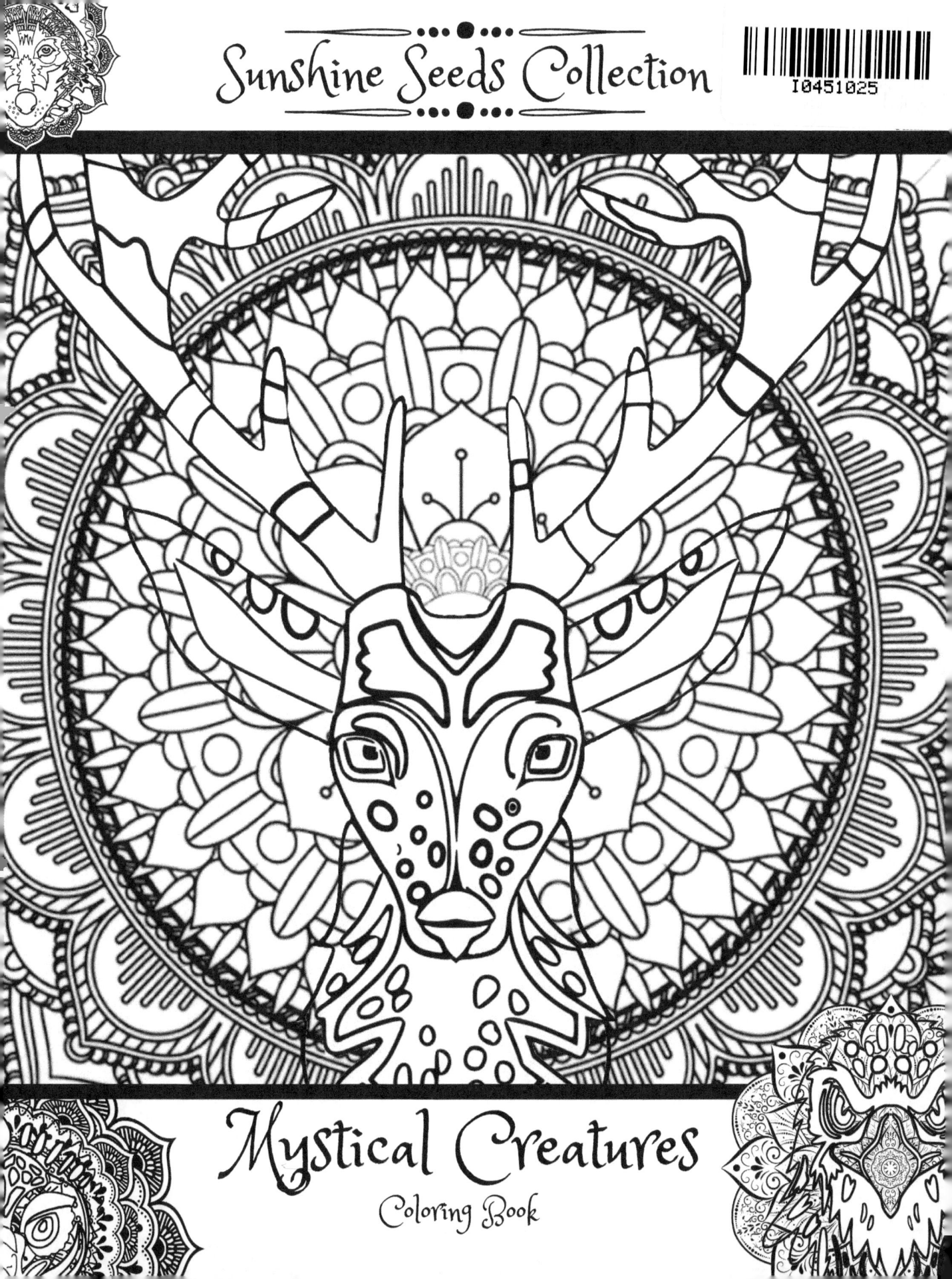

Sunshine Seeds Collection

I0451025

Mystical Creatures
Coloring Book

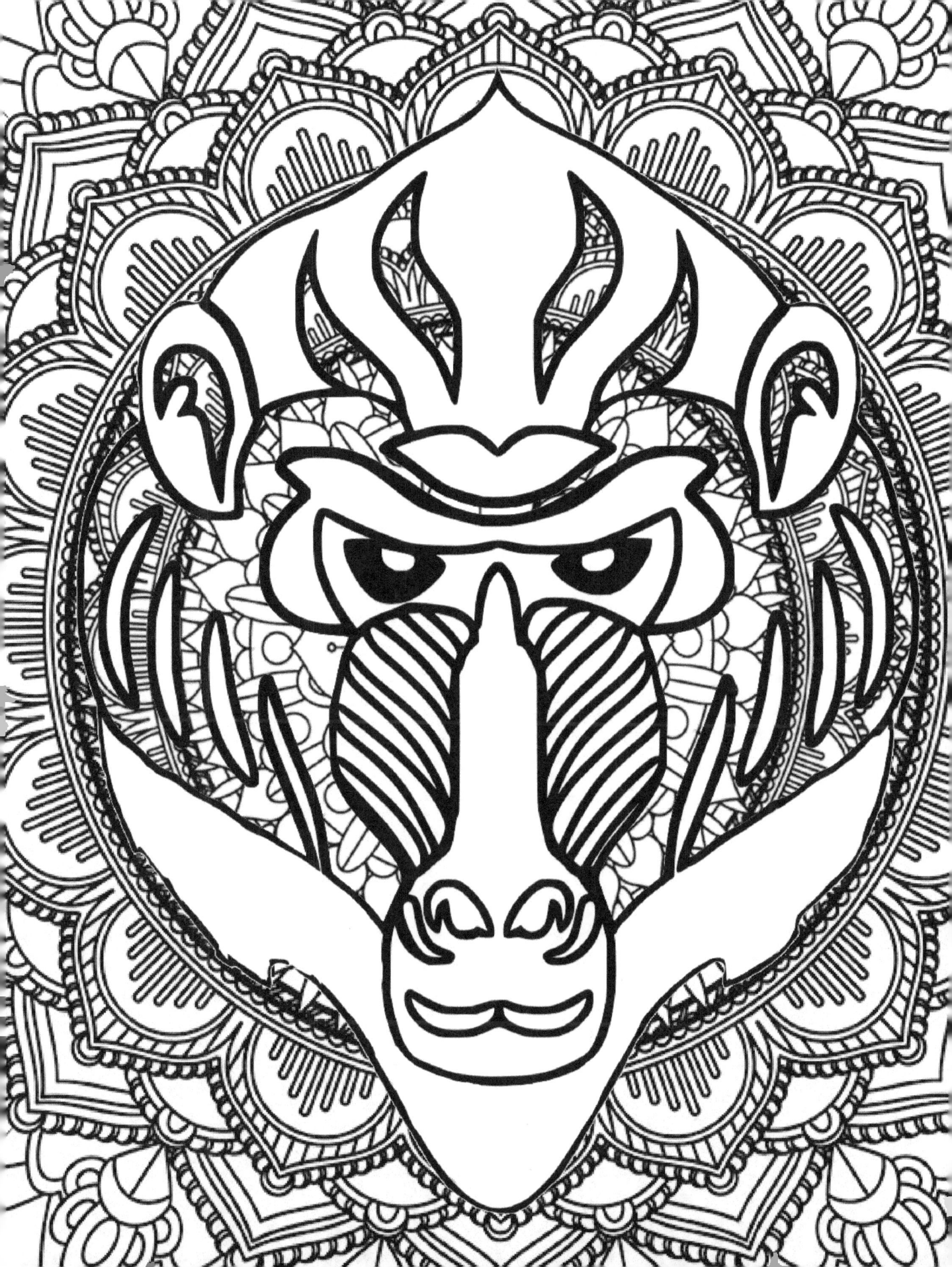

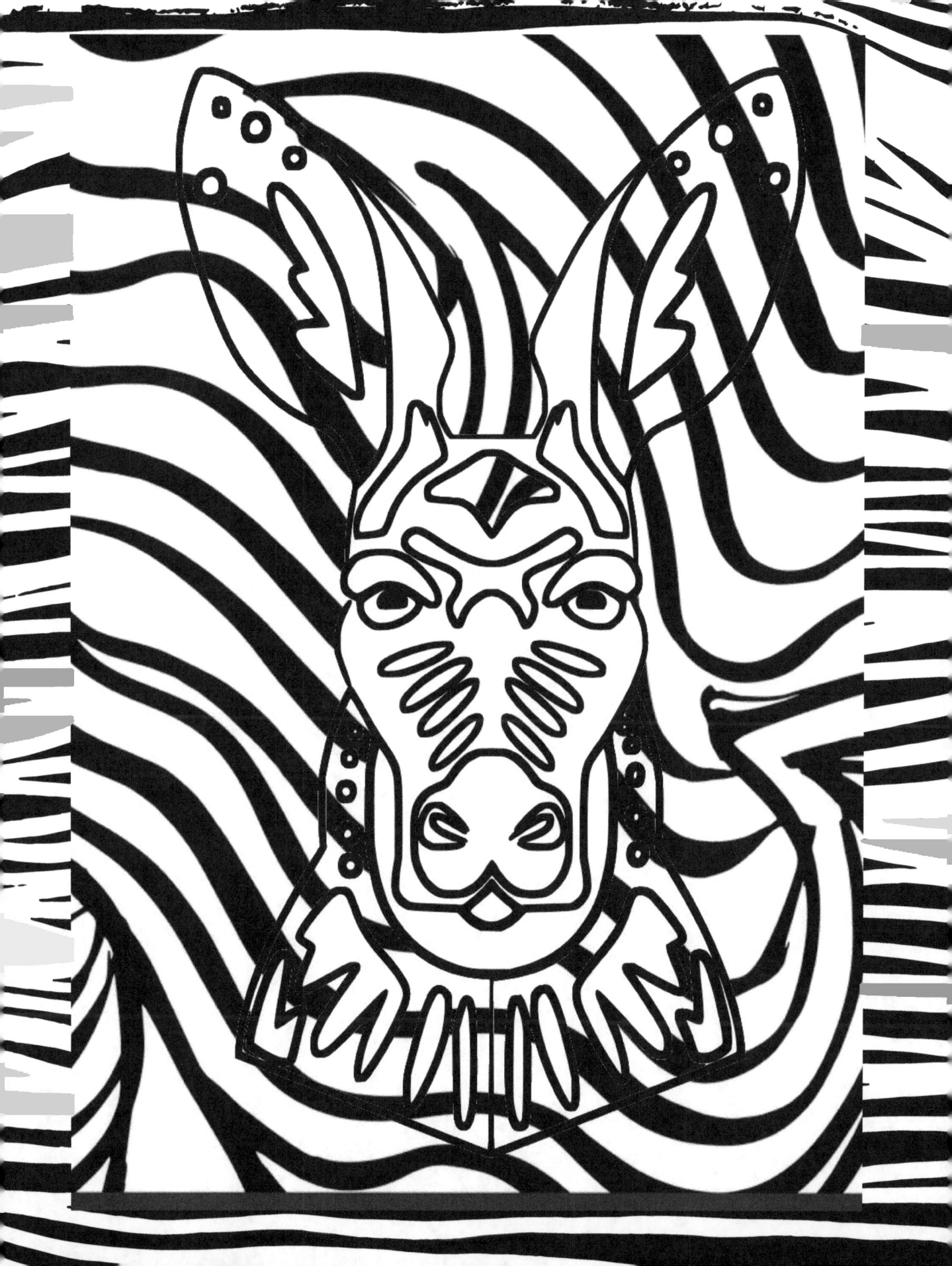

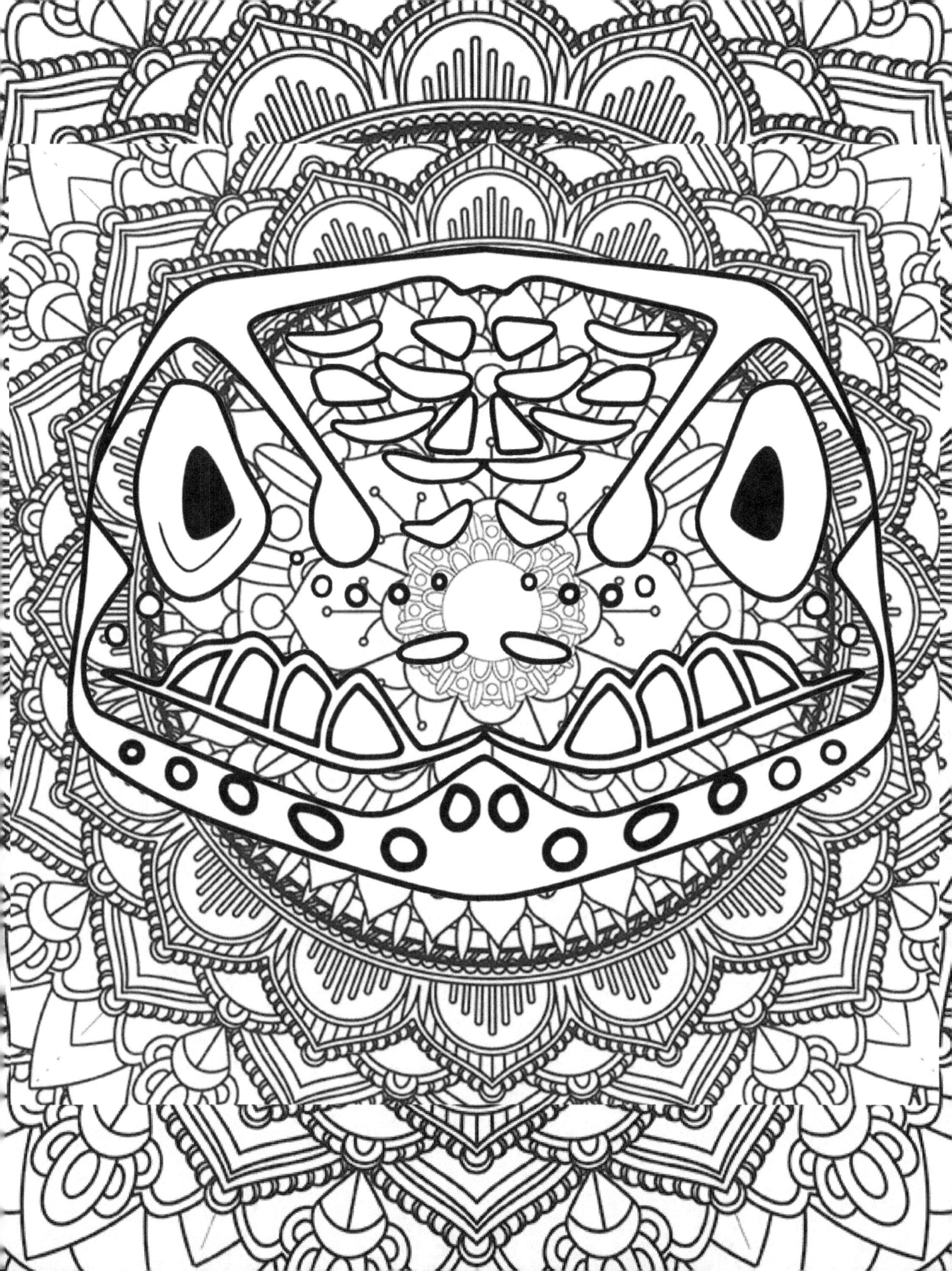

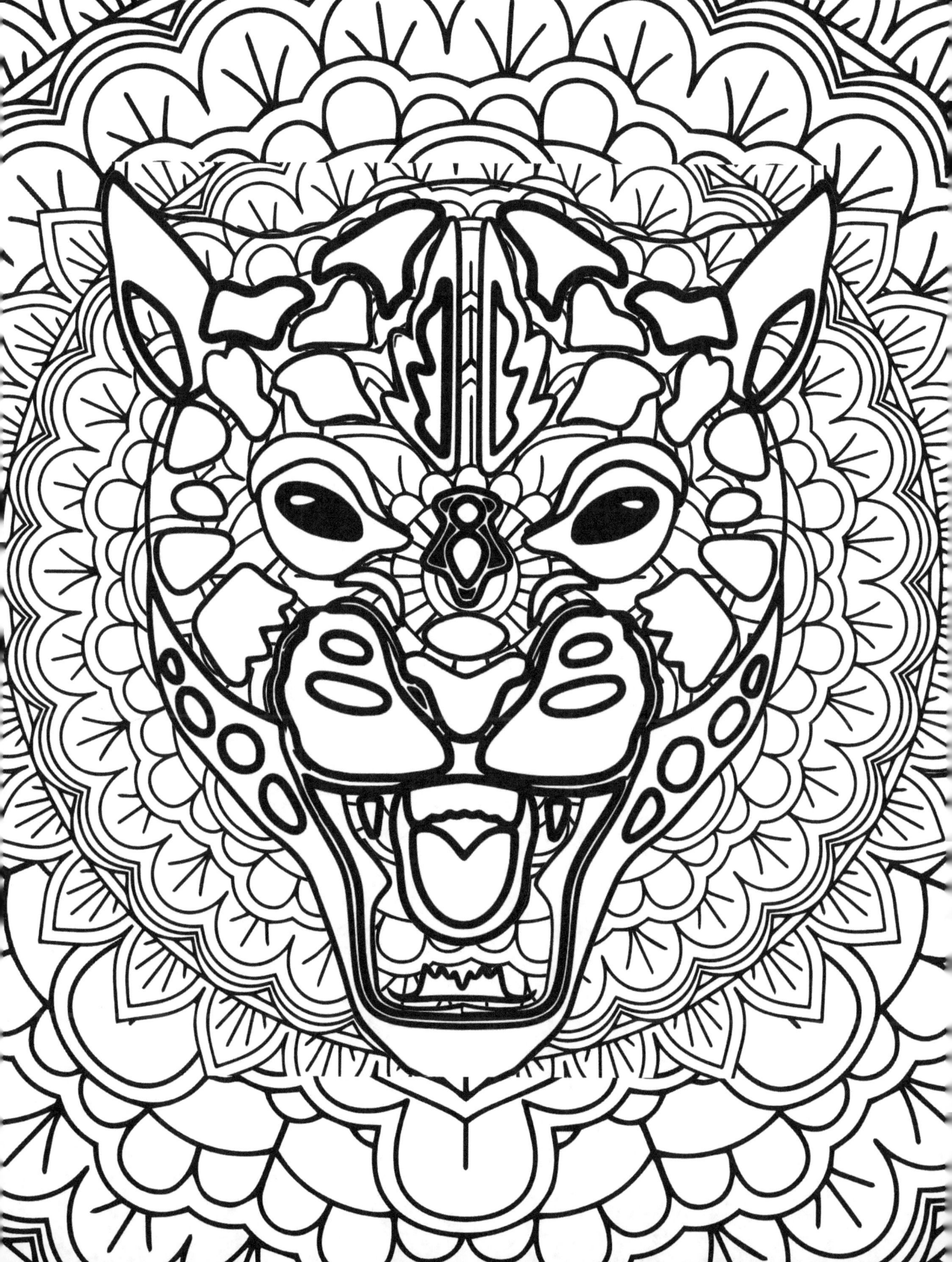

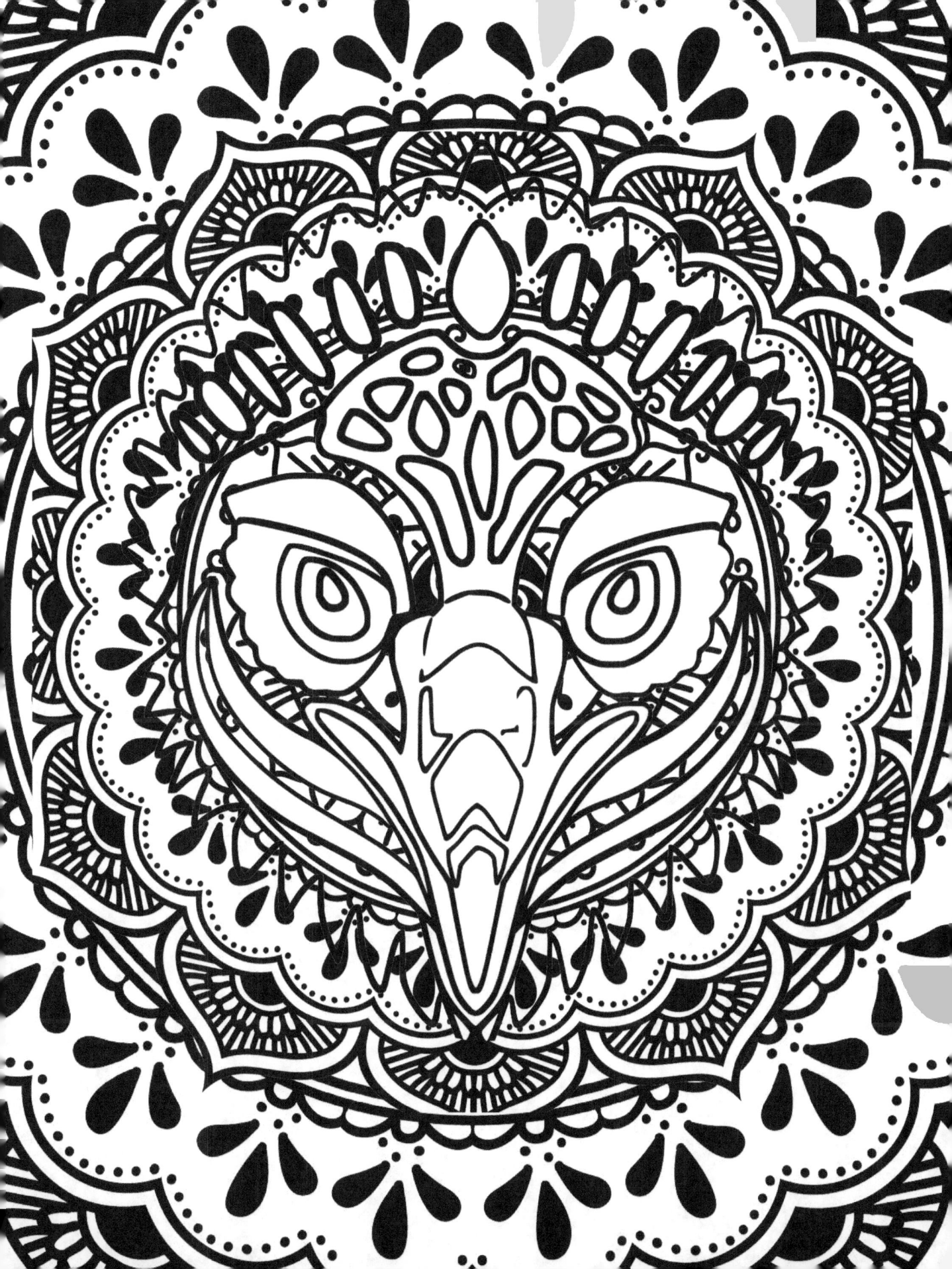

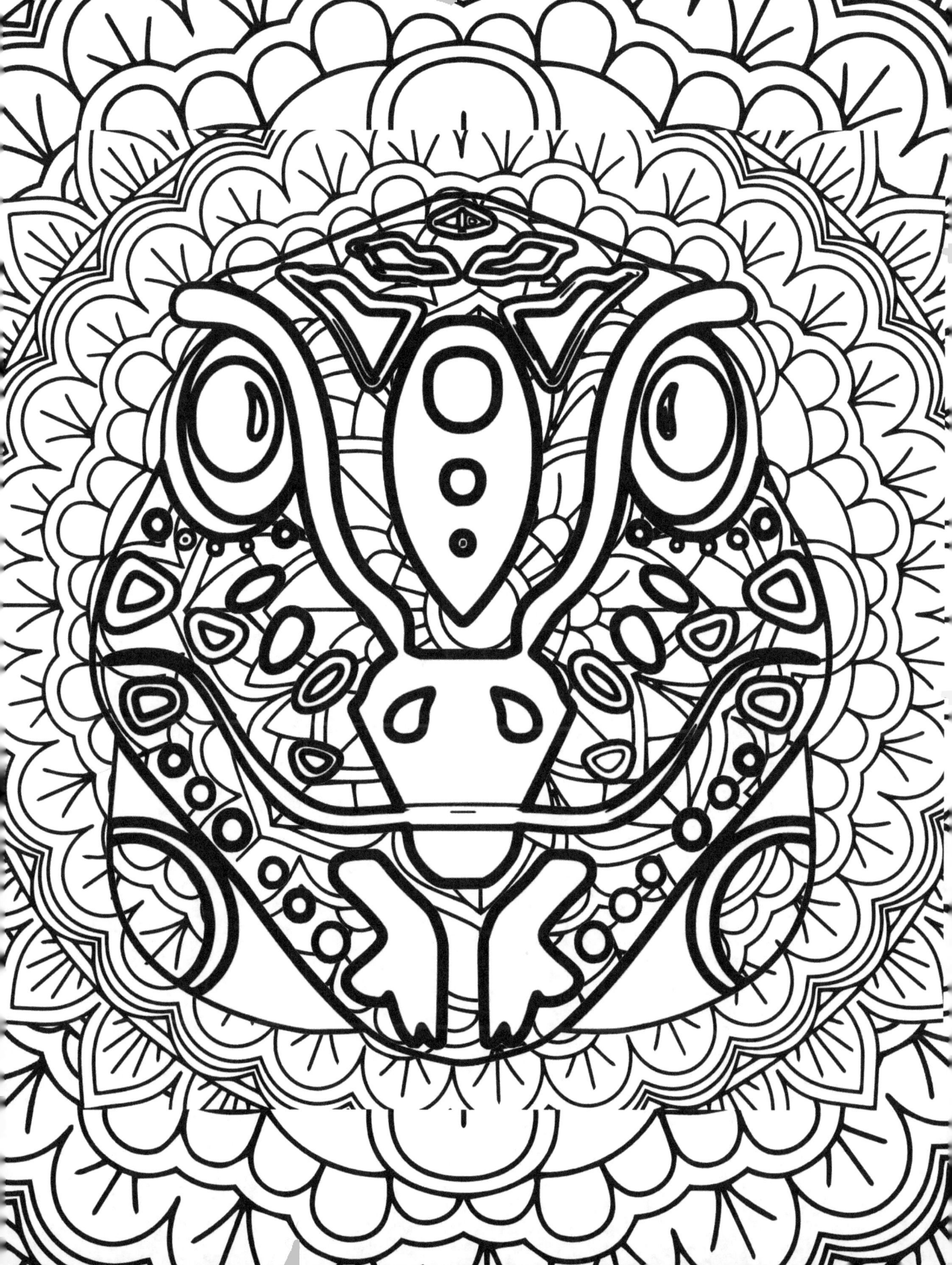

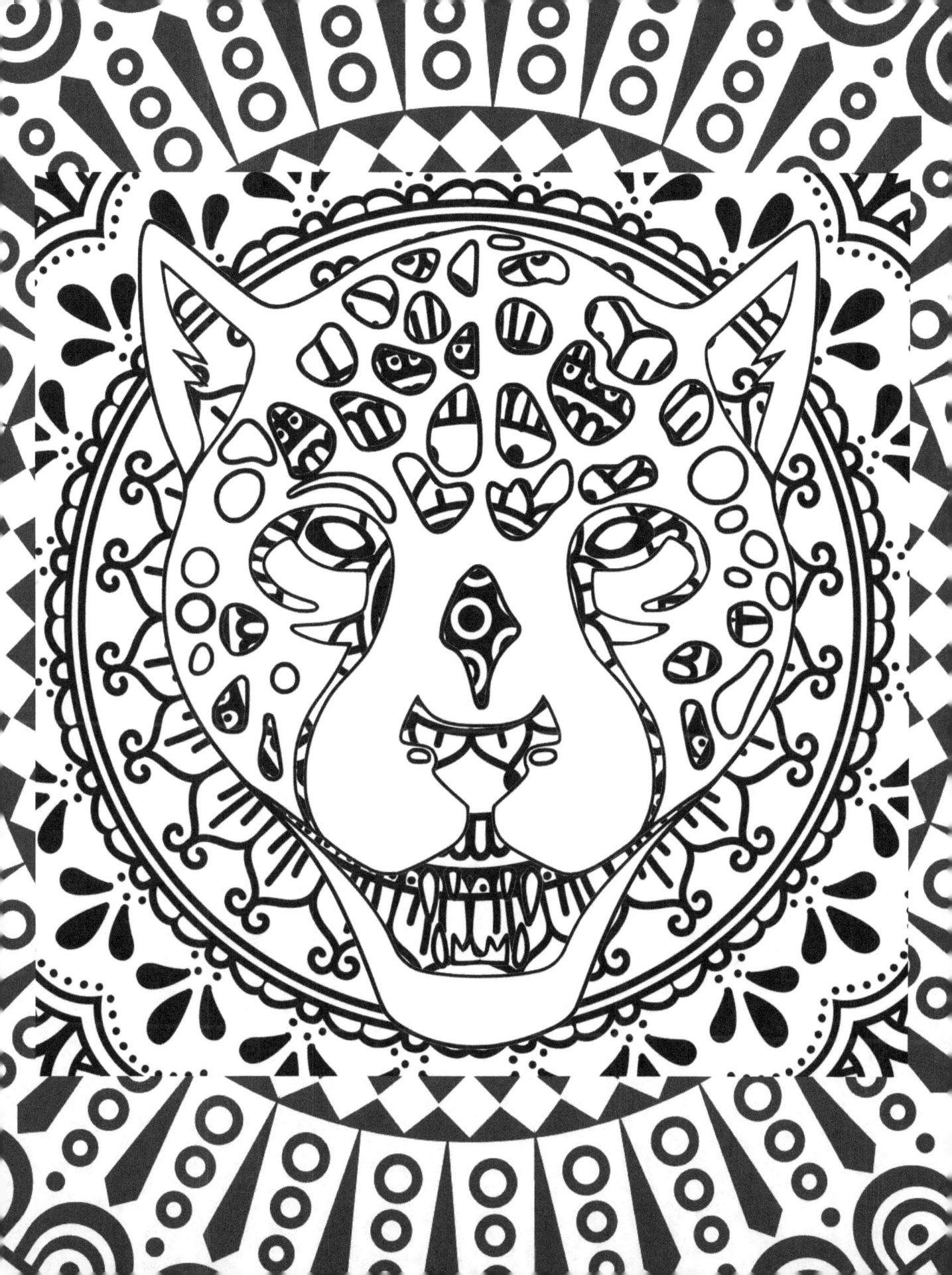

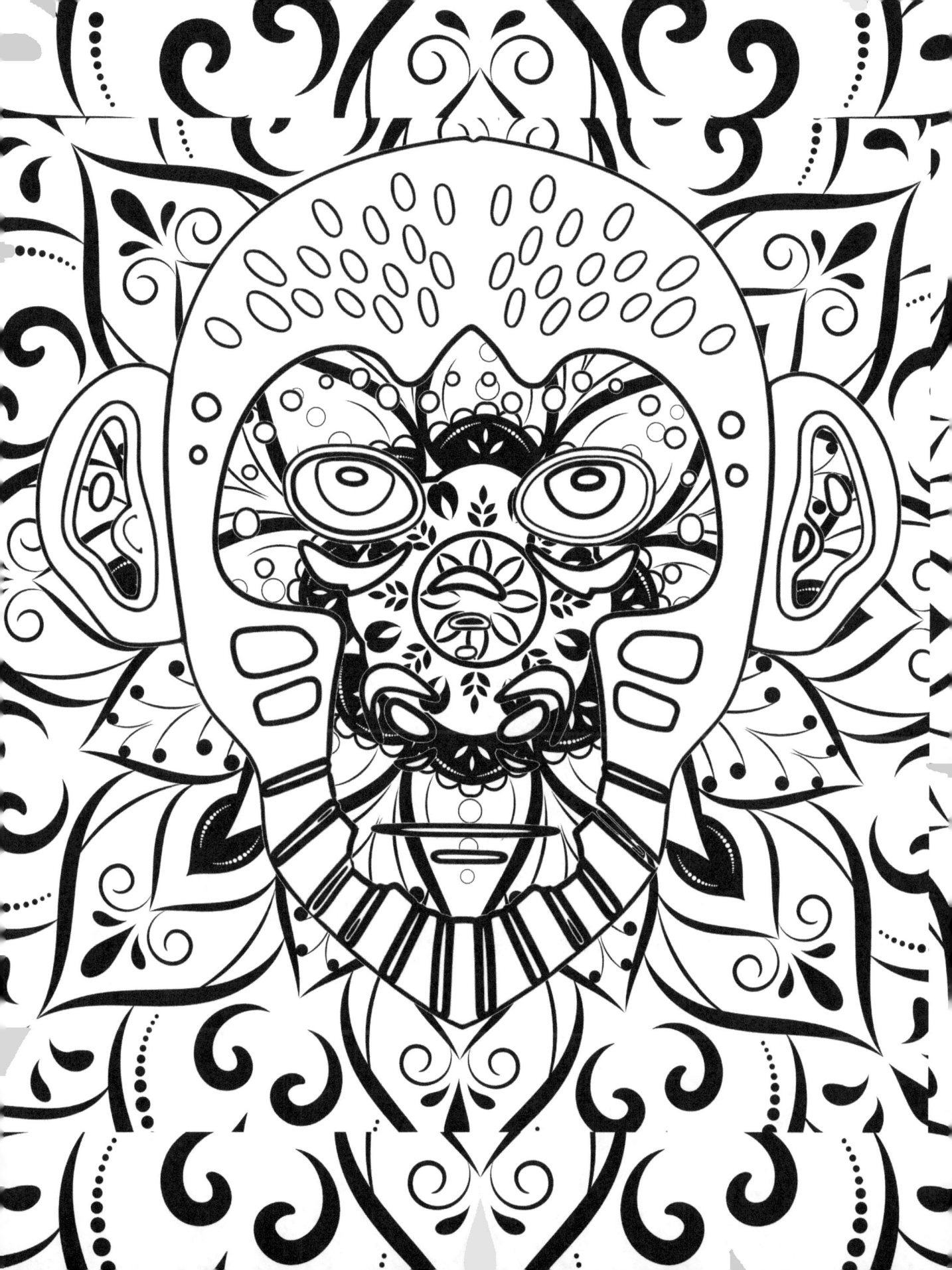

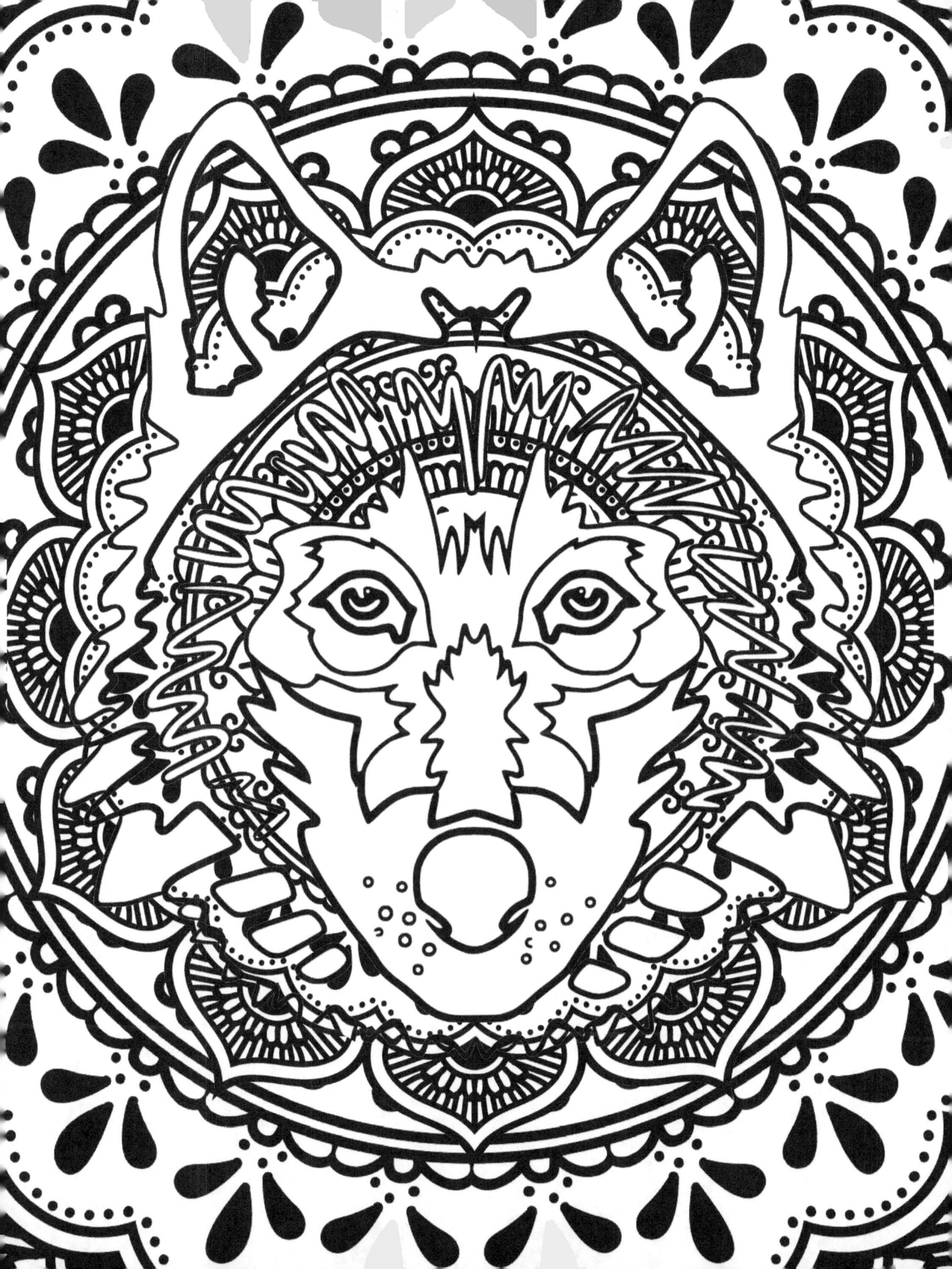

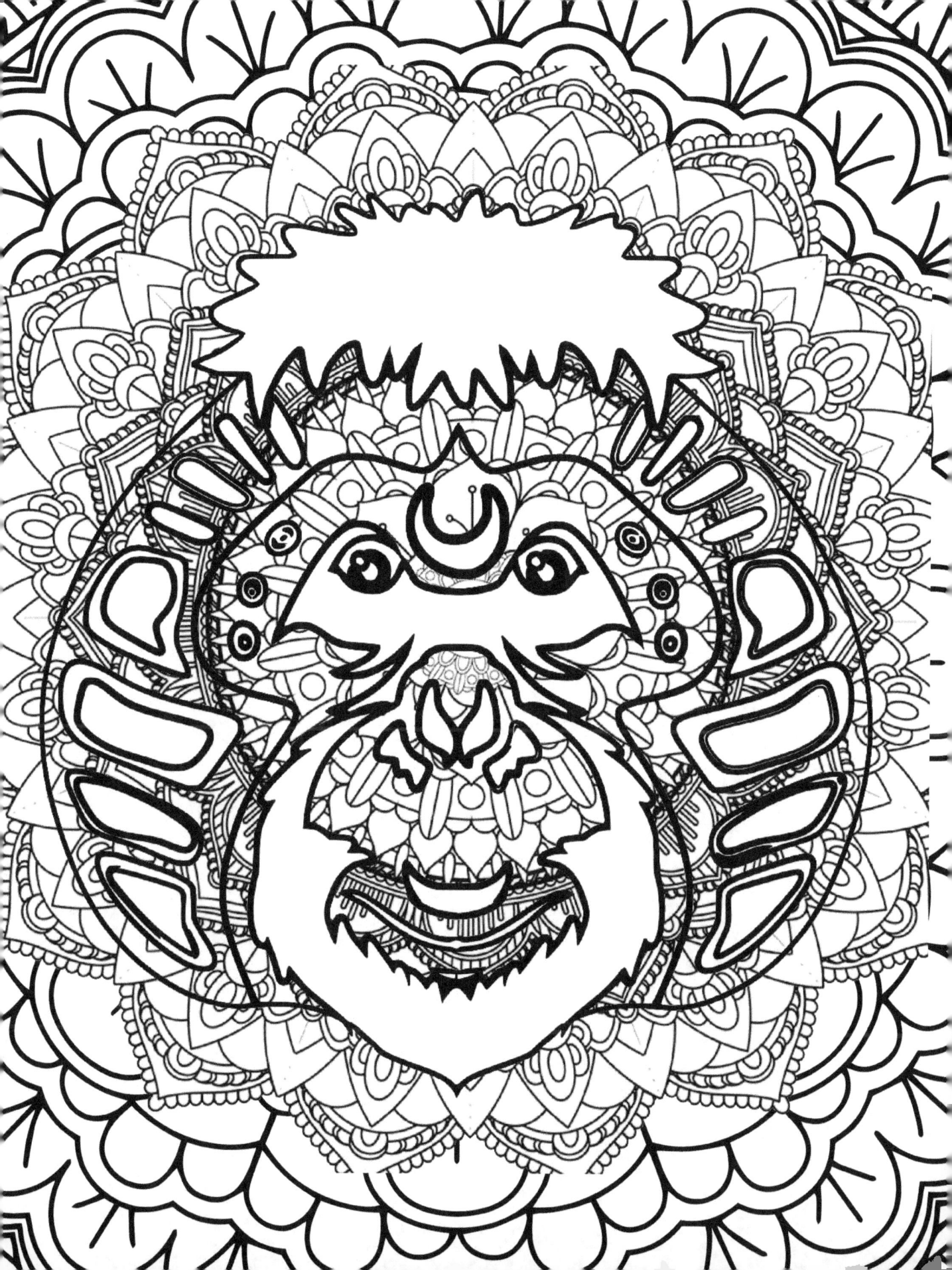

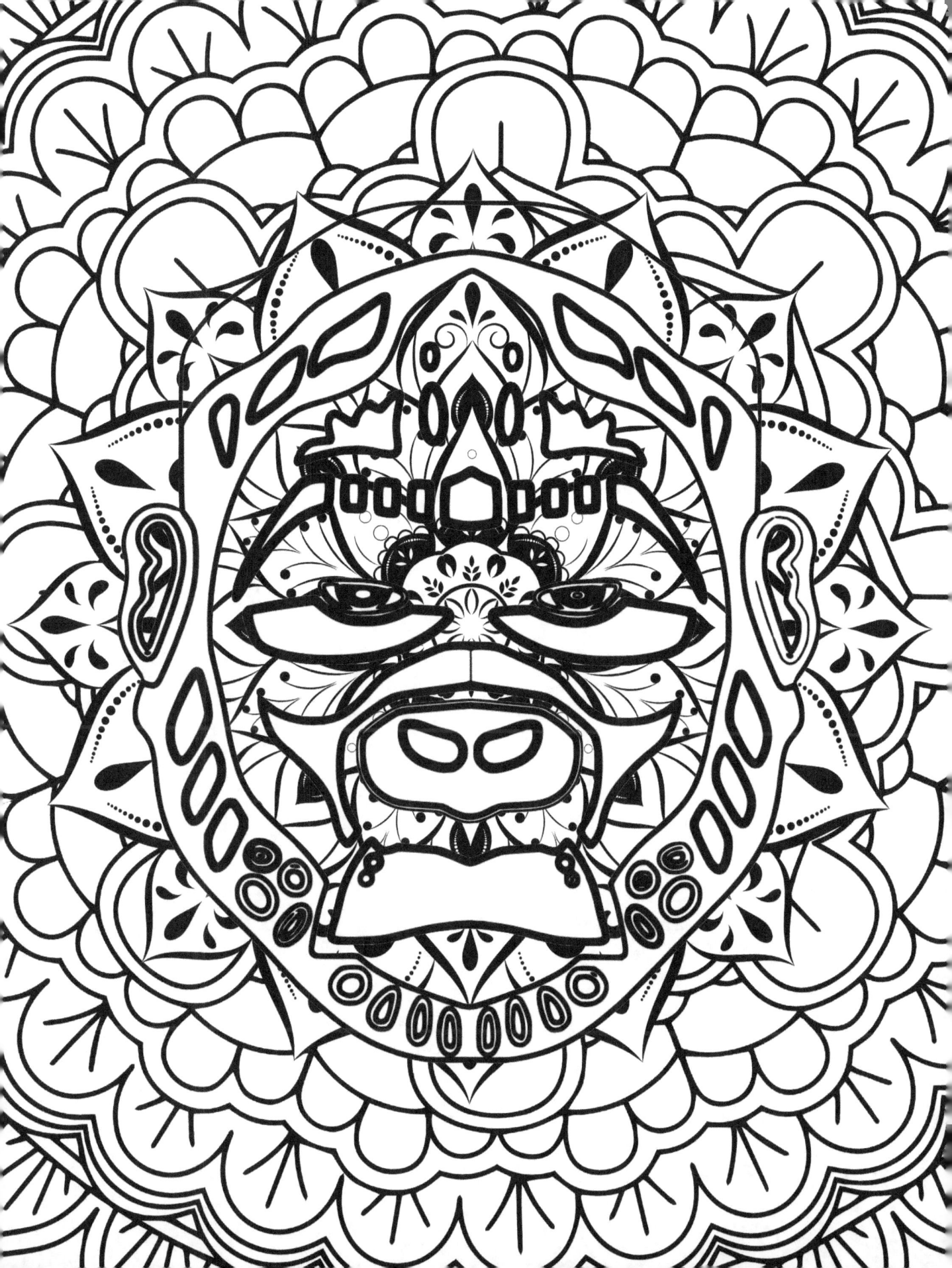

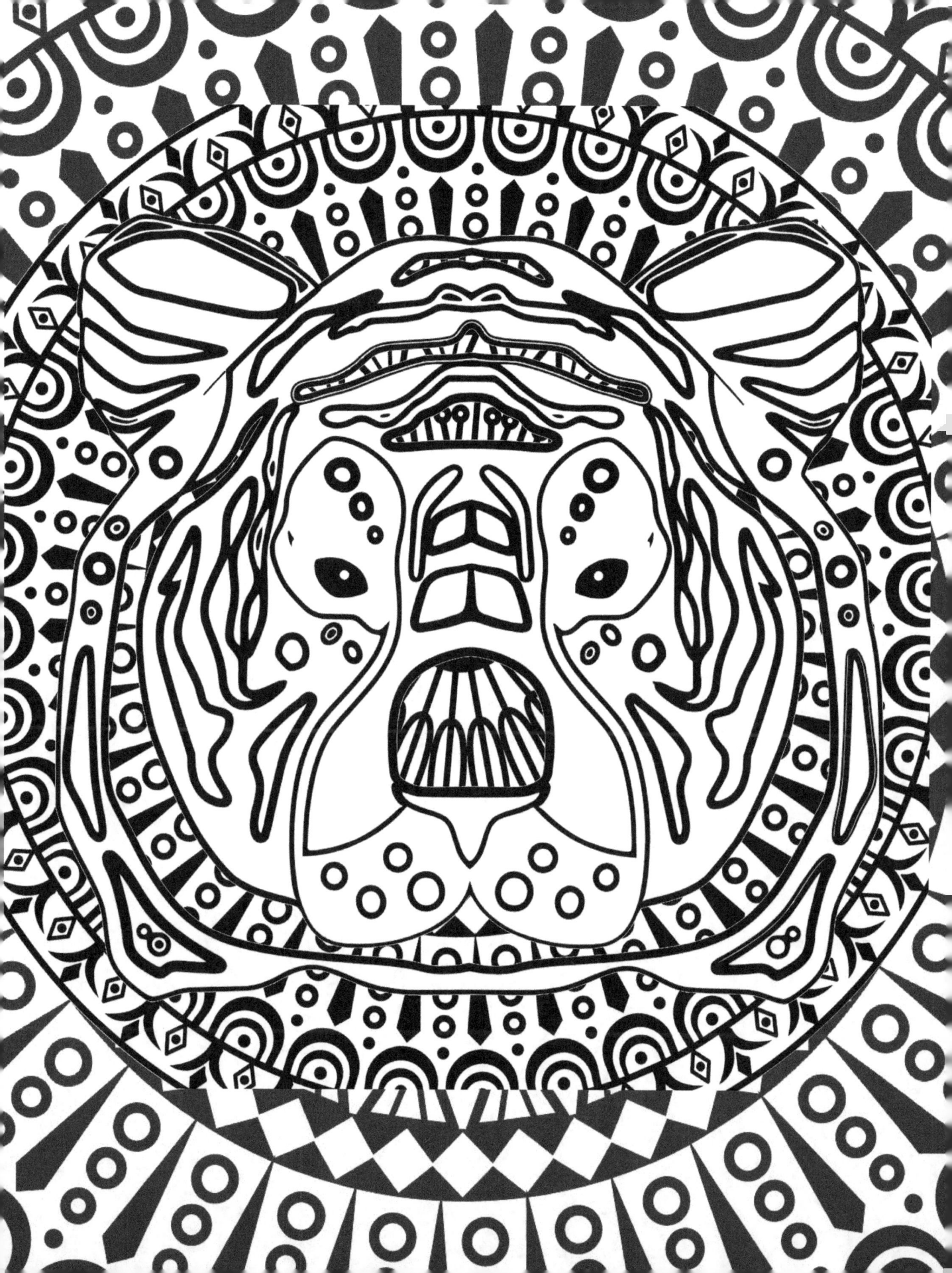

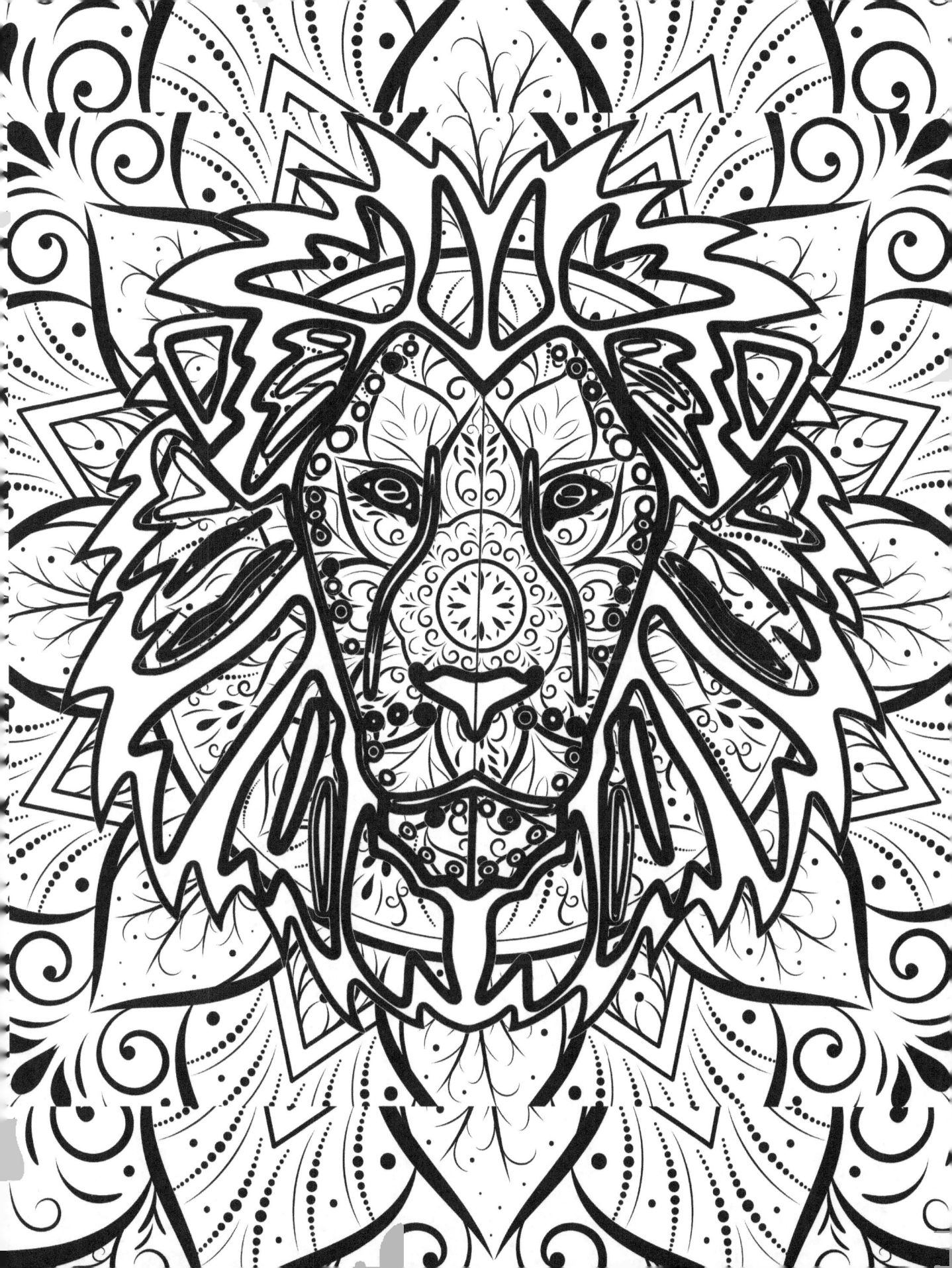

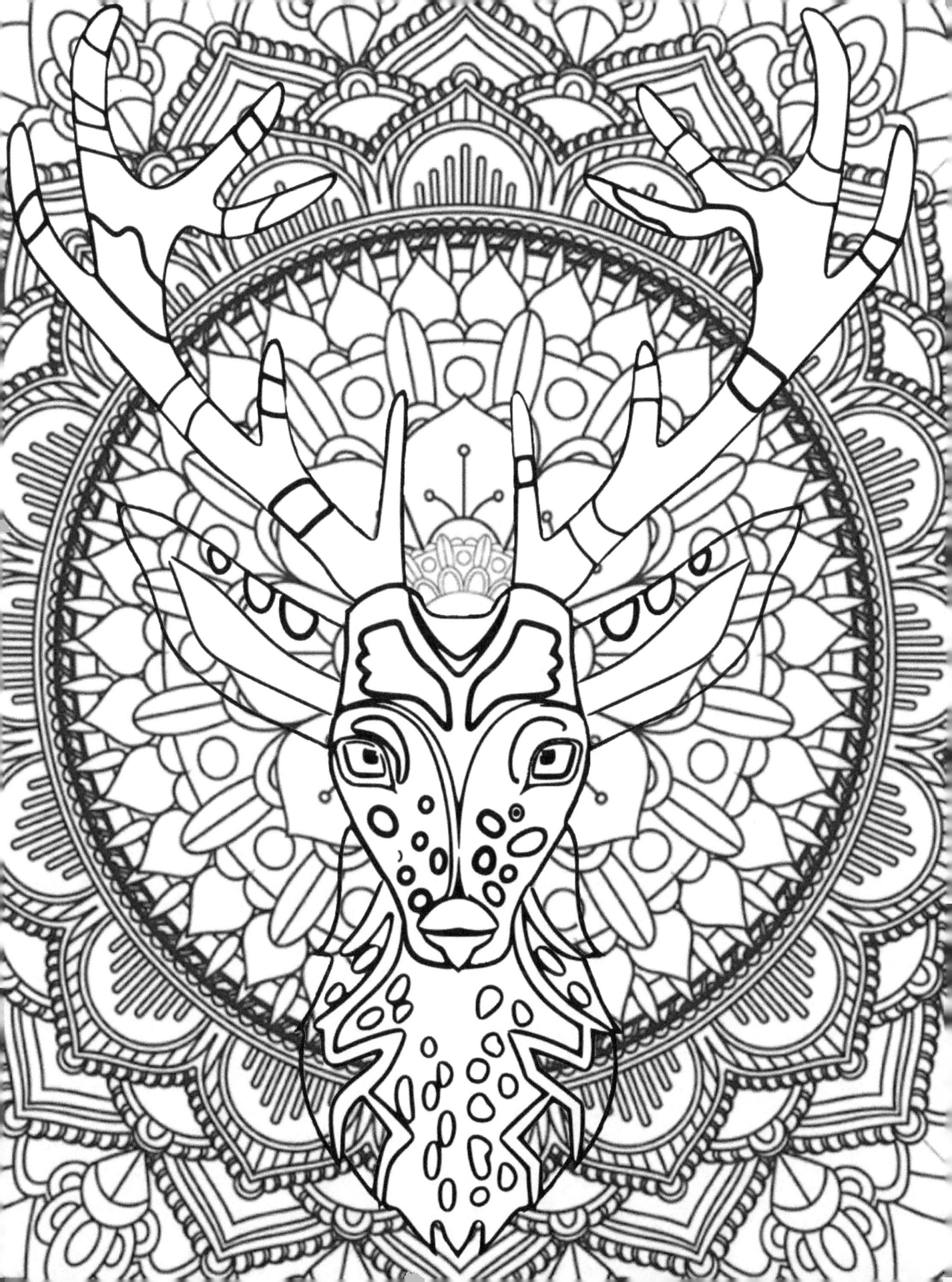

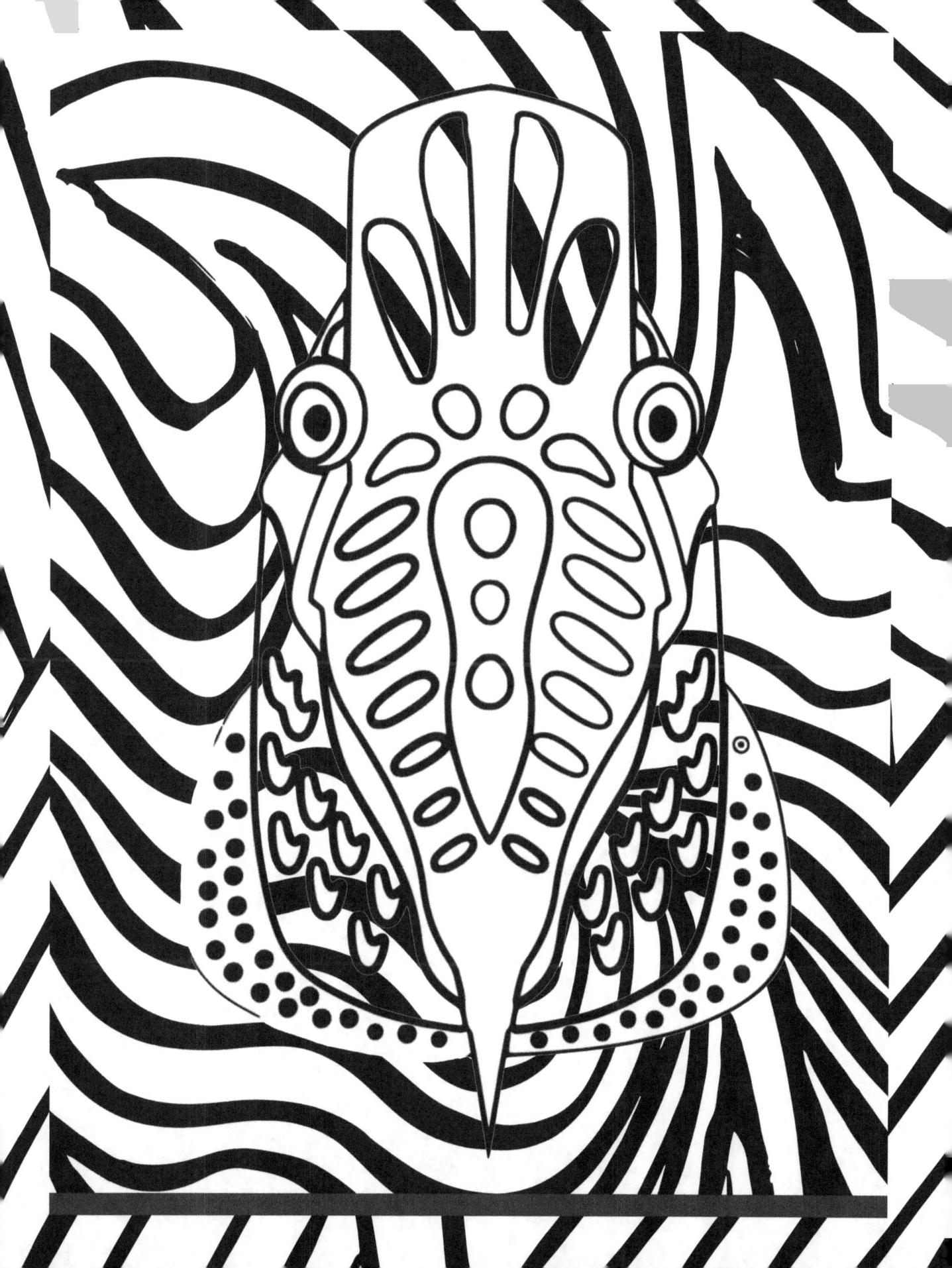

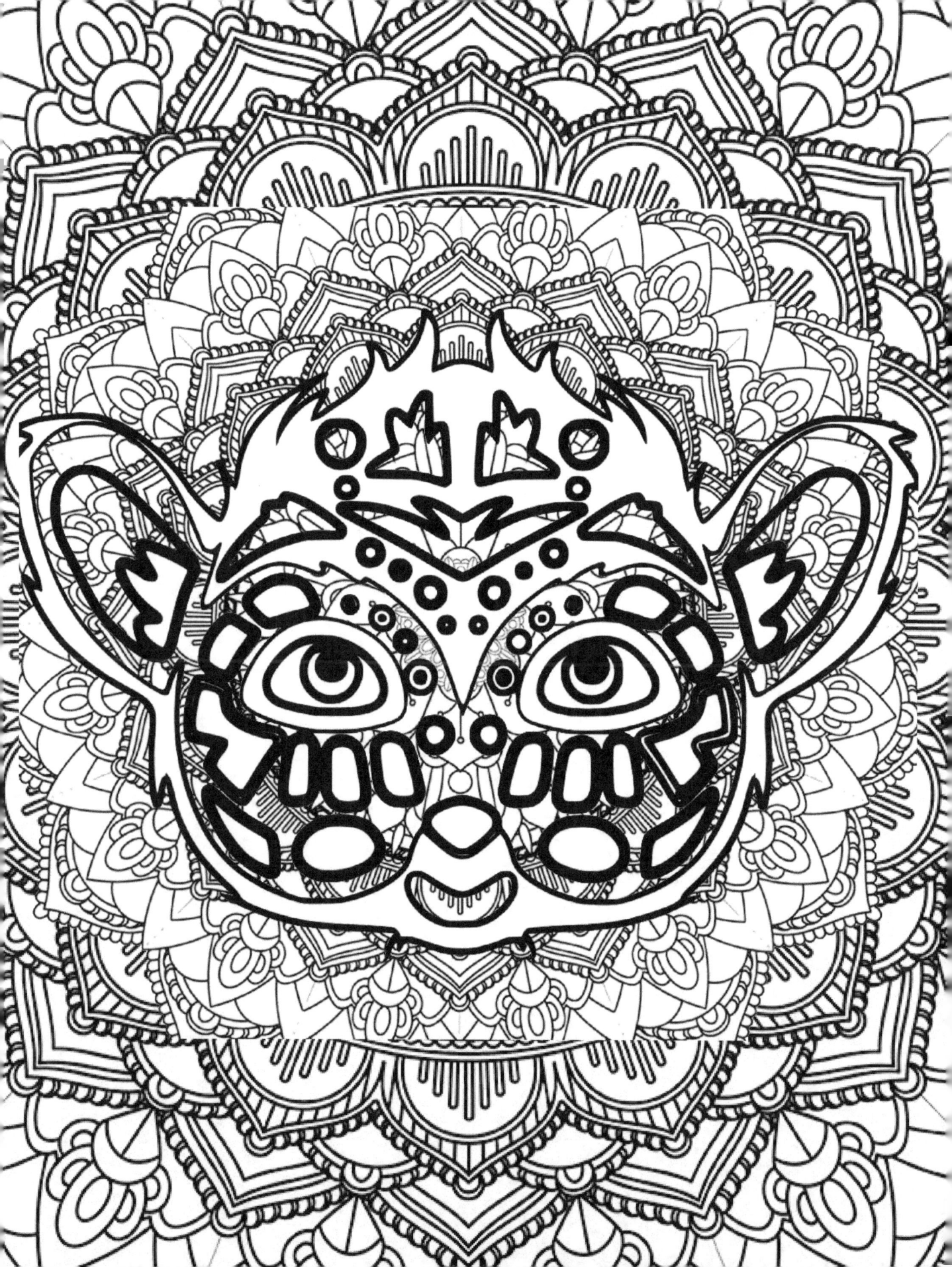

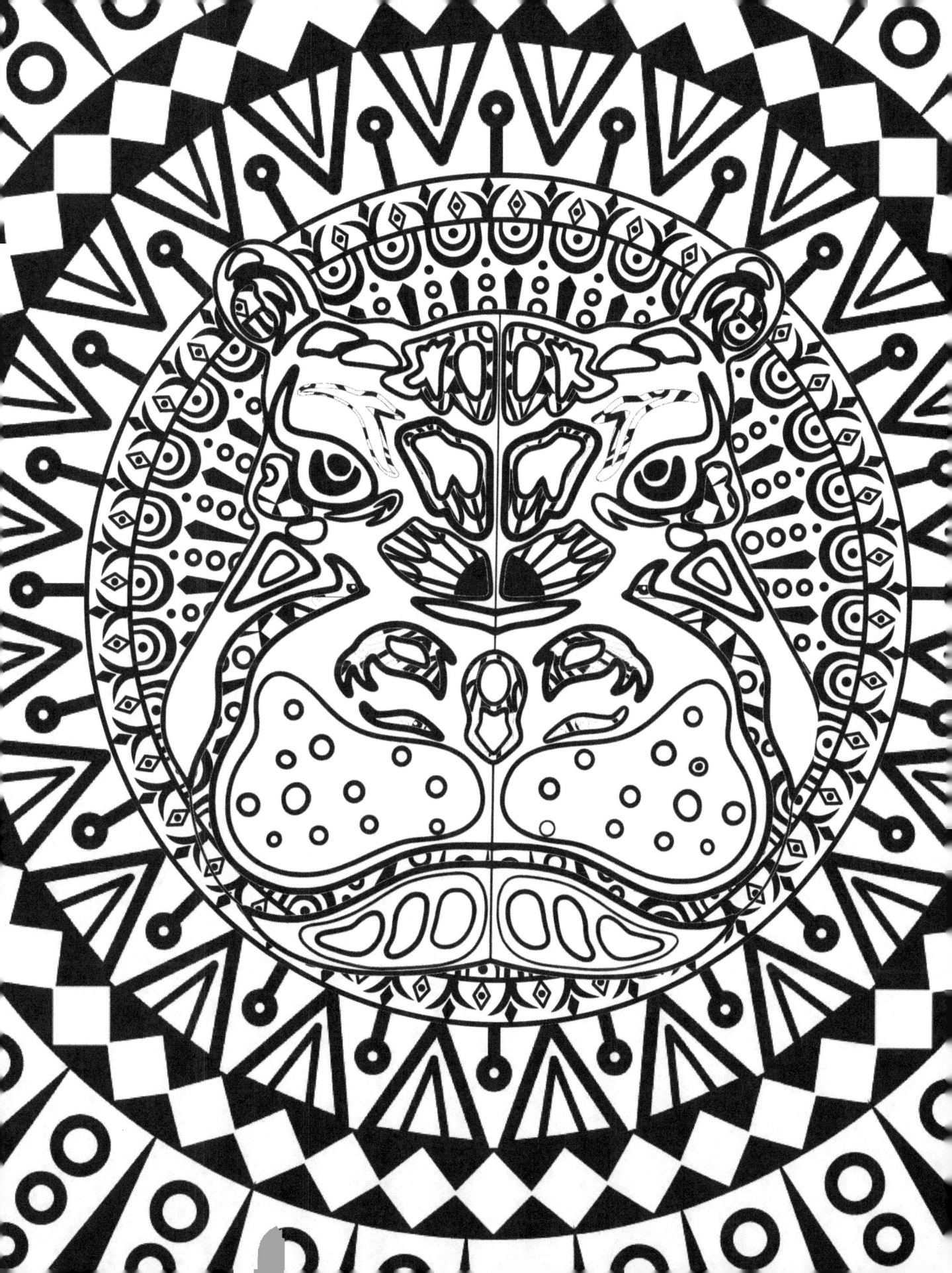

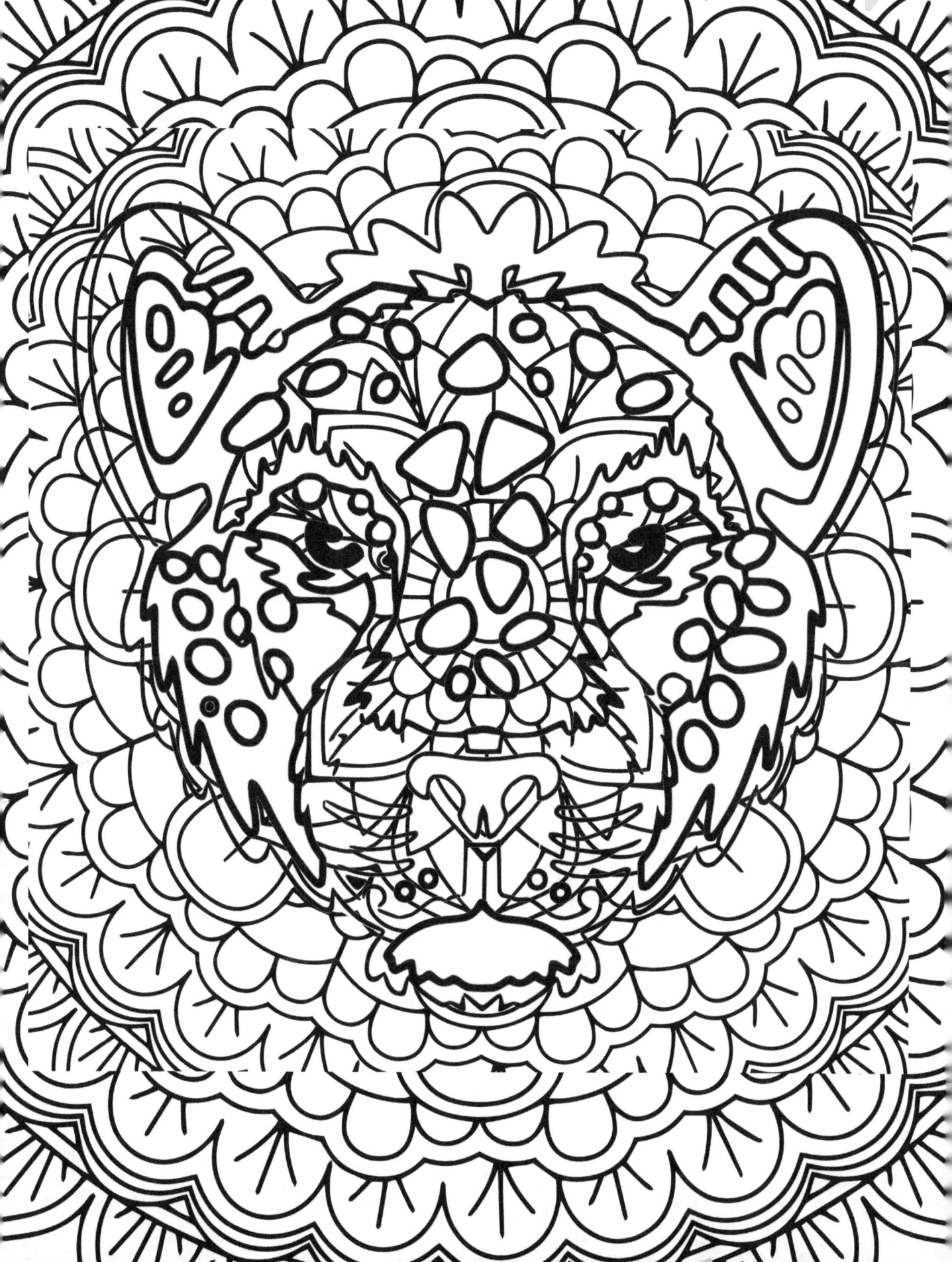

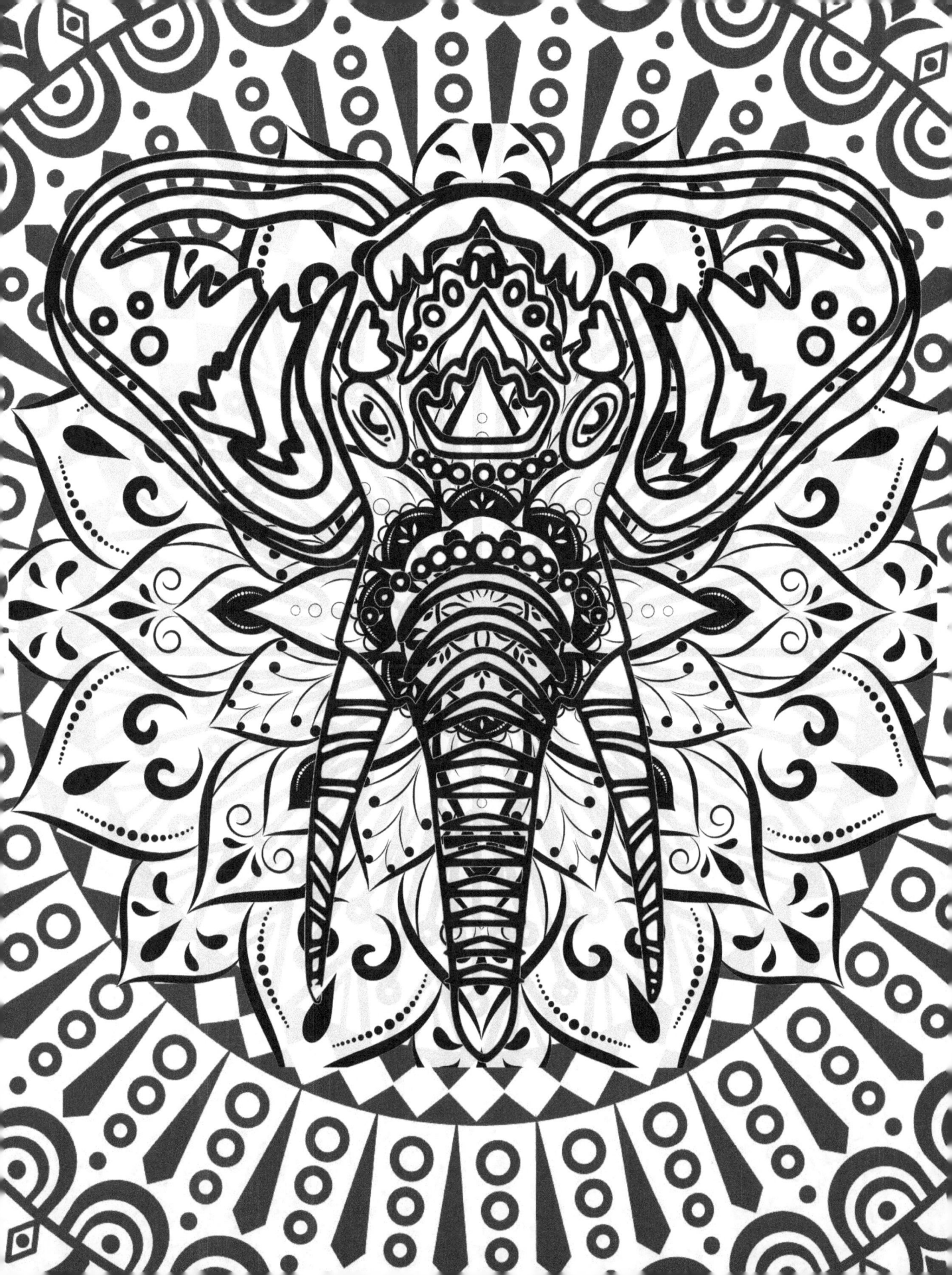

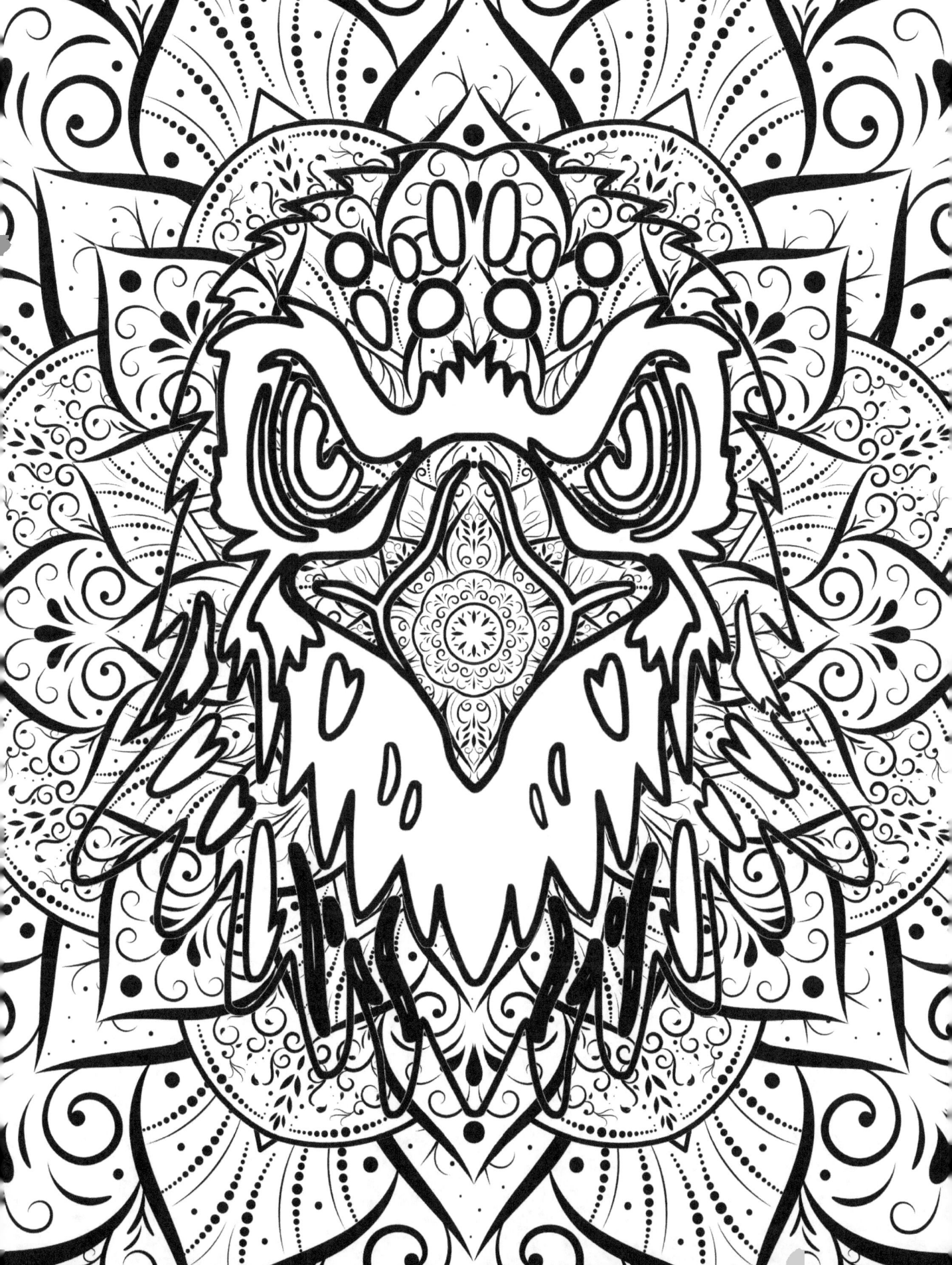

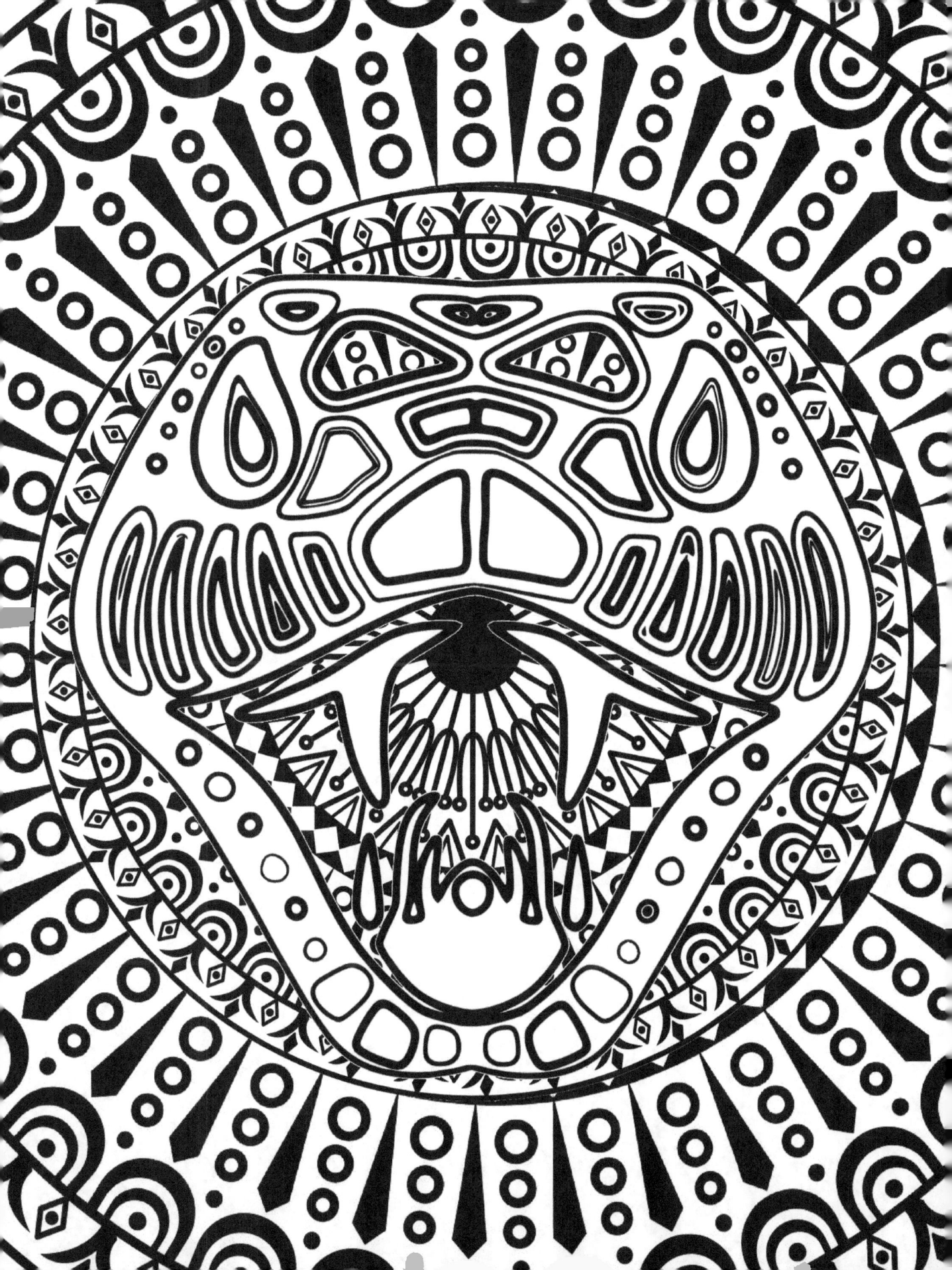

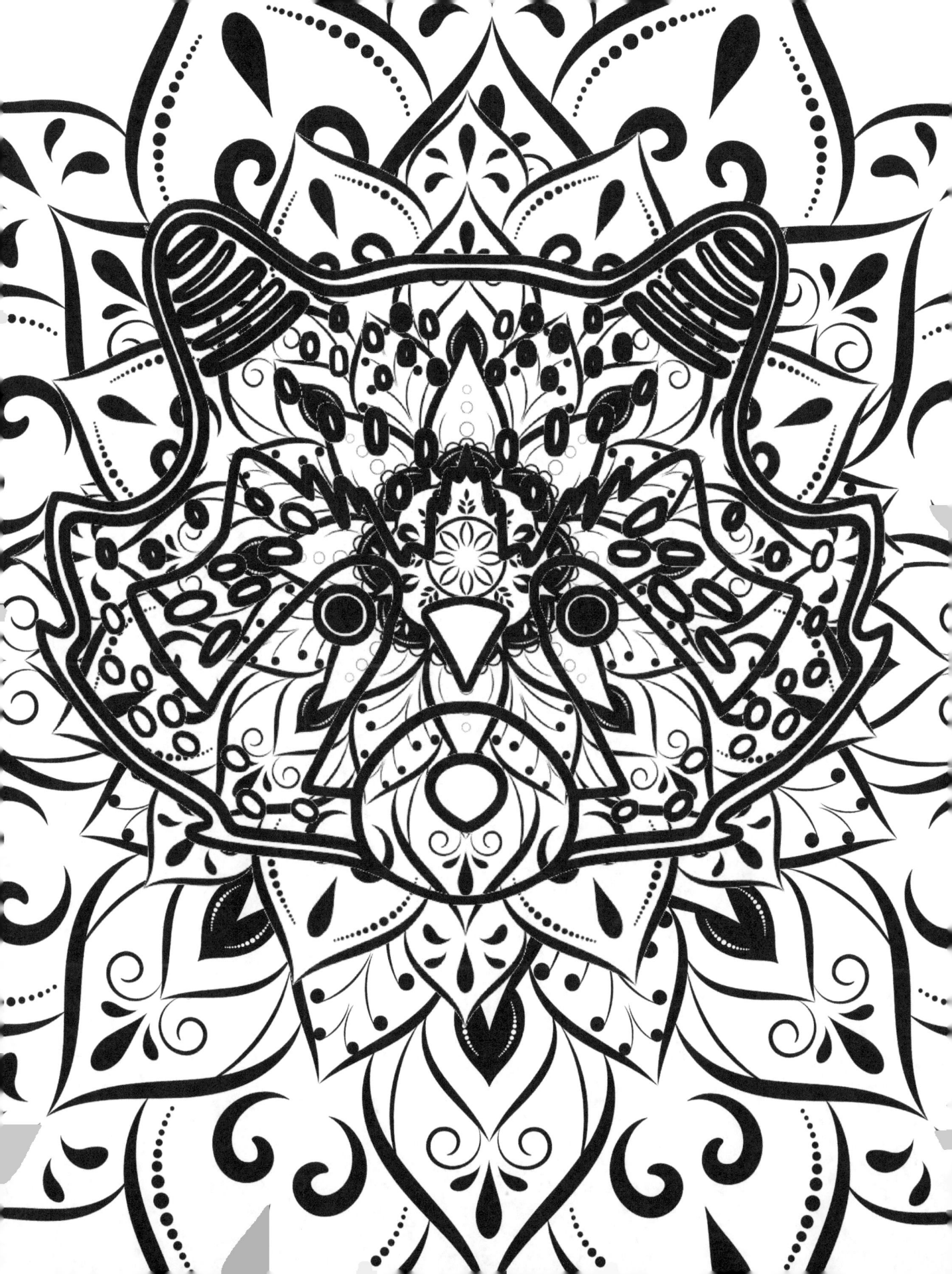

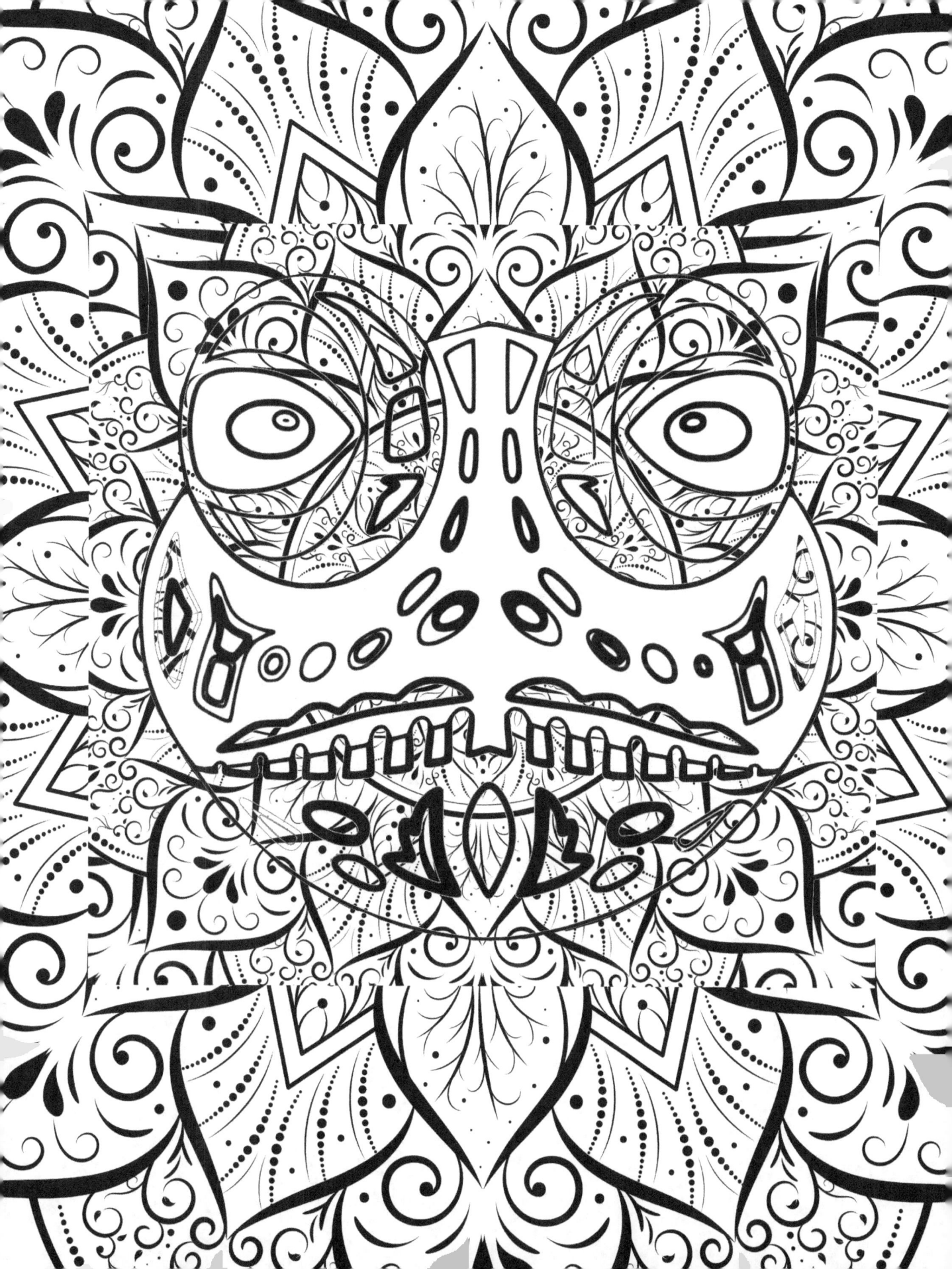

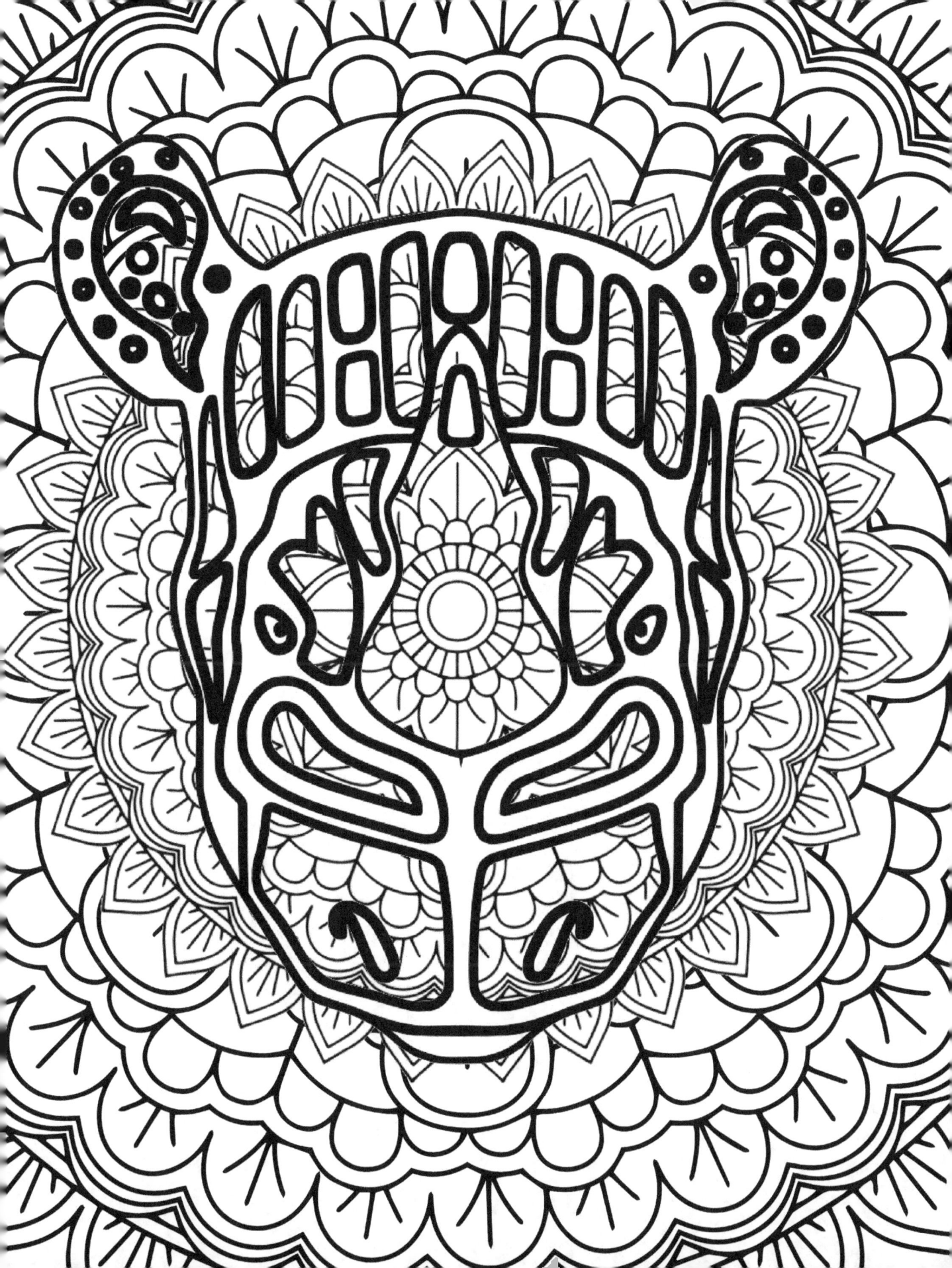

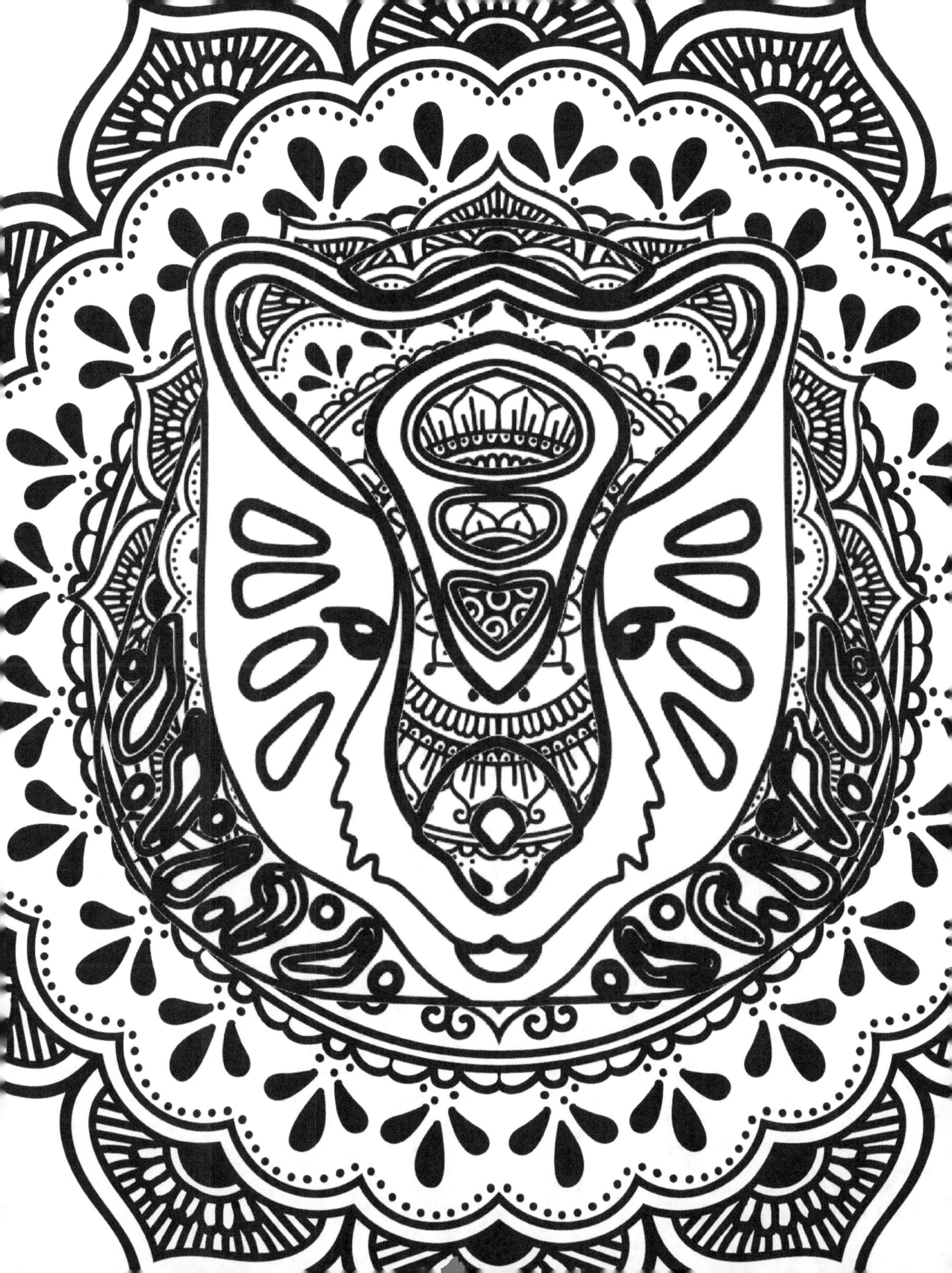

www.ingramcontent.com/pod-product-compliance
Lightning Source LLC
Chambersburg PA
CBHW081146170626

46809CB00011B/3165

* 9 7 8 0 9 9 1 0 3 9 9 7 5 *